THE GIRL IN THE FOREST

Bridgid Dean

Jolie threw down her apron and stormed out into the agonizing October sunlight, the busy pedestrian area of the small city funneling past her, her view fractured by tears. Behind her she heard her manager call her name once, in a tone that spoke volumes about how unreasonable he thought she was being. She didn't turn around. Hurrying past the library and the small park, she ignored the fact that she could hardly breathe, her throat constricted with the sobs she was trying to keep down.

    Damn that woman-damn the whole lot of them!

Finally, she had to slow down. Ducking into the organic food store she hid in the bathroom until her tears slowed and her breathing returned to normal. When she emerged the smell from the deli caught her off guard, causing her stomach to rumble. She did a mental inventory of what there was in her small kitchen and grimaced. When would she next be able to afford groceries?

Suddenly her anger at the customer, at her manager, began to pale in the light of a grim reality. Within a week, maybe two, she would be flat broke. Sighing with frustration, she admitted she should have just apologized. Everyone had known the woman was being a bitch. She could have just remade her order, bit her tongue, chosen her battles.

Instead she'd told the woman what she thought of her and quit her job. It hadn't needed to happen, wouldn't have happened, if not for the nightmares. Every night for over a month now the same awful dream had woken her. Even when she managed to fall back asleep something of the dream would linger through the day, like a veil that darkened her view of everything.

As though it hadn't been dark enough already.

In truth, she'd been weary and irritable for much longer than a month. Her mother had died in

April, bringing Jolie's world to a crashing halt.

Walking several more blocks, she was almost outside the shopping district when she saw the sign across the street. Illuminations, the sign read, with a picture of a hand next to the word, an eye staring forth from the center of the palm. She hadn't realized she was looking for it until she saw it. Waiting for a break in traffic she ran across the street, a strange flutter in her chest.

Inside, her eyes adjusted slowly. The sunlight seemed under clear instructions to wait outside and she almost sighed with relief to find herself in such a cool, dim space. The dark purple room was lined with bookshelves, a few glass cases surrounding the register displayed jewelry and crystals on dark velvet. A large woman in a flowing blue garment sat behind the counter, looking at a computer.

"Hi honey!" she said, turning with a smile towards Jolie. "What can we do for ya?"

"I'm not sure," Jolie cleared her throat, her voice scratchy.
"Just looking around, I guess."

The woman nodded.

"Downstairs we have all the new age books, upstairs is the used book section. Fiction, history, psychology, mythology..." The woman ticked the categories off on her fingers, then waved her hand as if it were all too much. She smiled.

"Jamie's up there. If you have any questions, he can probably help."

Jolie held onto the chipped banister as she climbed to the second floor at a geriatric pace. She wasn't sure exactly when the headache had started, but it had passed the stage where it might be ignored. Her head pounded to the rhythm of her heart, so she moved slowly, carefully, trying to ease the pain. At the top of the stairs she turned left, ducked into the room labeled Folklore/Mythology. It was a small room, the windows made of a foggy, textured glass, as though it had once been a large bathroom. Where the linen closet might have been there was a little nook in the wall and an old armchair tucked inside, covered in discolored gold velvet. Seeing no one in the room, she sank into the chair and groaned softly.

She sat with her eyes closed for several minutes, long enough for the chill damp to penetrate her thrift store cardigan, her worn jeans, and her combat boots. She pulled her long dark hair into a pouf on top of her head and started to massage her temples.

"Want some aspirin?" a man asked, making Jolie start.

Leaning against the bookshelf across from her was a man in a threadbare T-shirt, his sinewy arms covered in tattoos that crept down over his fingers. His hair was equal parts black and silver, a bit long and very unruly. His nose was crooked, as though it had been broken at some point. His eyes were huge, dark, but friendly looking.

"Yeah," she finally managed. "Aspirin would be great."

He set down an army green canvass backpack, pulling out four books, a pouch of tobacco, and what looked like a deck of cards wrapped in a silk handkerchief before finding the small plastic bottle.

"Here we are," he said, handing it to her.

"Are you..." she sought for the name the clerk had mentioned, "Jamie?"

"Mmmhmm. Did Bella want me to help you find something?"

Jolie popped two pills in her mouth, tried to swallow. Jamie offered her a bottle of water. She hesitated only a moment before nodding her thanks and washing the pills down.

"I don't really know what I'm looking for."

He sat down cross legged, leaning against the end of a shelf.

"I can probably help you narrow it down."

She opened her mouth, then closed it again, looked down at her hands in her lap.

"Go on," he said. He had a low, soft, voice. She looked up and he smiled at her, head tilted as though curious. It had been a long time since anyone had given her their complete attention in this way.

"Really," he said, "I won't judge."

"Well, I keep having this dream," she began, and then hesitated as the memory of it made her stomach twist.

"Reoccurring dreams can be very important," he said.

"In it I'm by this lake in the woods near my apartment. I'm sitting on a dock that juts over the water, and as I'm staring at this strange statue across the lake the dock comes unmoored. About the time I realize that I've floated to the middle of the lake I see a storm rolling in- suddenly the water is electrified and I'm miles from shore and about to capsize!" She offered an embarrassed grin.

Jamie cocked his head to one side, studying her. "There are lots of books on dream interpretation here, but maybe you should consult the cards. I could do a reading for you."

She shook her head, feeling her cheeks grow warm under his scrutiny.

"It's the figure in my dream that I keep thinking about, the statue of a woman looking at me over her shoulder. I can only see her back, and the side of her face, but her gaze seems alive, like she's just hiding in the statue. Her back has this big hollow in it, shaped like a tear. I guess I was just wondering if there was any mythology or folklore about a creature like that." She'd been staring at her boots through much of this speech, but when she looked up he had pulled his legs into his chest, his chin resting on his arms as if deep in thought.

"We could pull out some books on folklore, fairy lore, but honestly, I've read most of them cover to cover and it doesn't sound familiar. Which doesn't mean it isn't symbolic as all get-out," he paused. "Sounds like something's troubling you, at any rate. I'd journal about it, at the least."

"Good idea," she said, standing quickly and blinking back tears that had come out of nowhere. It'd been awhile since anyone had spoken to her this kindly, she realized. The thought made her want to cry even more.

"What woods were you referring to? Just out of curiosity."

"The Grenzie Forest," she said, clearing her throat, "a little north of here. It's a beautiful place, it bums me out that my dreams about it have been so frightening. I love to sit by the lake across from the old cottage and just sketch or think."

He nodded slowly. "I know the area, but I've never seen a cottage."

She shrugged. "It's a big forest." Wandering over to the next shelf she steeled herself for her next question.

"How do you like working here? I don't suppose you all might be hiring?"

"I wouldn't know, I don't actually work here. Bella, the woman downstairs, is a dear old friend. She lets me read tarot cards here, in the little room at the end of the hall. You'd have to ask her." He nodded at her chest. "Bagel Brothers not working out, Jolie?"

She looked down. In her rush to leave, she'd left her name tag on. She took it off, walked over to the little waste bin and dropped it in.

"Very much not working out. I quit, actually. Just about half an hour ago."

Jamie smiled slightly. "I bet there's a story there."

Jolie picked a random book up, opened it and stared at a page, unseeing.

"I don't know if it's much of a story. I haven't been in the mood to deal with people. And this morning I had a woman yell at me because I put half 'n half in her skim mocha latte. So I told her she was a heartless bitch, and that there were more important things in this world than her waist line. And I walked out."

Jamie's grin widened. "Give as good as you get, I always say."

Jolie smiled even as she shook her head. "It was stupid, I can't afford to be out of a job."

"Come on, how old are you? Surely mom and dad'd pitch in a bit during a rough patch...

She shook her head, adamant. "It's not like that. My mom died four months ago, I dropped out of college to take care of her. My dad left for the west coast the second he could with his new girlfriend. He'd always seemed so infatuated with my mom, almost uncomfortably so, but as soon as she was in the ground he seemed like a different person. Couldn't wait to get on with his new life. Seems like I'm just an unpleasant reminder of the old."

"Damn, Jolie. I'm sorry about your Mom." He didn't look uncomfortable, like he was anxious to change the subject. She'd gotten used to the way people cringed away from her grief.

"I got an idea," he said, his smile so lit up that she responded in kind before even hearing it. "My friend Greta's talked about hiring someone. I'll call her today, mention you. She needs help before the Halloween festival in two weeks."

His grin took on an impish quality as he looked at her sideways. "You'll have to come see me tomorrow to find out what she says."

She blushed, grinning despite herself.

"OK," she said, trying for something like indifference. "Tomorrow afternoon."

§

Bella smiled at her the following afternoon as she walked in the door.

"You were in here yesterday, weren't you?"

"Yeah," Jolie said. "I, uh, came to see Jamie."

"Ohhhh." The way Bella said the word made Jolie cringe.

"About a job. He said a friend of his might be hiring." Jolie found she was moving towards the staircase.

"I wonder if that's Greta. She's up there with him right now, I think he's reading her cards so you might have to wait. He doesn't have a whole lot of friends around here. We grew up a couple of hours away, I've known Jamie since high school." Bella glanced at the stairs, lowered her voice. "He's been through some rough times these past few years, but I think he's coming out the other side. Always had a big heart, that's why I let him stay here. He's been there for me over the years."

Jolie opened her mouth, then shut it, unsure how to respond. "It's certainly kind of him to help me find a job. I really need one," she replied, after only a brief pause.

Bella looked as though she were about to say something else when a customer walked in the door.

"He'll be in the room at the end of the hall," she said, then turned to greet the newcomer.

Upstairs Jolie read the sign on the closed door: *Reading in Session. Please Do Not Disturb.* It was written in black sharpie marker in a style vaguely resembling calligraphy. Ducking into the fiction room, she ran her hand along the spines of the books as she made her way to the tall window overlooking the street. The afternoon sun poured in thick as sap, time suspended in the golden stillness. Closing her eyes, she watched the light from behind her closed lids, feeling as though she was floating on it. She heard the sounds of the bell ringing over the front door, the clack of the register shutting, as though from some great distance. Finally, she opened her eyes and, moving into the stacks, sat on the floor to peruse the lower shelves.

A few minutes later she heard the creak of

Jamie's door opening, followed by the low murmur of conversation. Then a striking blonde woman entered the room. Crouched down, the woman didn't notice Jolie as she passed, her glittering black skirt rustling against the black tulle petticoat beneath. She looked out the window, peering up and down the road before she nodded and walked briskly from the room, her shoes clicking down the stairs. Jolie released the breath she had been holding, slumping against the shelf behind her.

She did not think of herself as insecure, generally. She had an attractive, if somewhat slight, figure. She knew her thick, wavy brown hair was her best feature, as it softened a face that had often been called "serious." She'd been told her green eyes were pretty. But the blonde woman Jamie had just been speaking with was stunning.

After killing a few minutes reading she convinced herself to get over it and knock. Inside, Jamie was reading a book in one of the ubiquitous vintage arm chairs. He smiled and motioned for her to come in. The room was tiny, the couch opposite Jamie almost filled one wall, and faded Indian print tapestries covered every surface. Colored Christmas lights, tacked up close to the ceiling, were the main source of light besides the one small window, which was covered in a torn bit of purple paisley cloth.

"Perfect timing," he said, putting his book down on the table.

"I just got you a job, if you still want it." He smiled, then cocked his head when she didn't immediately look happy. She forced a smile.

"That's wonderful. What's the job?"

"Greta owns a bakery. She was just here. It's too bad you didn't get here ten minutes earlier, I coulda introduced you two."

Jolie sat down on the faded Victorian settee.

"And she's willing to hire me, just like that?" She had not, until now, considered how odd this was.

He waved this aside and she noticed, for the first time, the tattoos on his fingers.

"She wants you to start tomorrow. The Halloween festival is in two weeks, she has a huge order to fill for it. She needs to get someone trained beforehand. I'll write down the address for you," he said, pulling a piece of notebook paper and a black sharpie marker out of his pack. "She asked if you could be there at seven thirty."

Jolie nodded and Jamie glanced at the worn deck of cards on the table. "You want your cards read while you're here?"

Jolie's mind flashed back over the past year of

her life. She shook her head.

"I don't think I want to know about the future. If I'd known a year ago what was ahead of me..." she trailed off.

His dark eyes seemed sympathetic as though, without knowing the specifics, he understood the sentiment.

"You can always change your mind," he said, handing her the address.

She folded it slowly, tucked it in her purse.

"I am interested in the cards though." She hesitated, hoping she wasn't being too transparent. "Would you teach me about them?"

He nodded, reaching over to shut the door.

"I'll show you the first one, anyway. You should get a book and a deck, though, if you decide you're really interested." He took his cards out and fanned them, face up, in his hand. Pulling one from the fan, he lay it down on the tattered silk handkerchief that covered the table.

"The Fool," Jamie said. His hand hovered over the card a moment, and she saw tattoos across his fingers were the phases of the moon. In the glow of the Christmas lights Jolie looked at the card; an optimistic young man, dog at his heels, walked dangerously close to a cliff edge.

"This is the first card in the deck, or the last. It's numbered zero." He looked up at her through his heavy brows, head tilted to one side. He was compelling looking, if not actually attractive, she finally decided, for the first time feeling the loneliness of this new town as a blessing. There would be no one to explain her strange attraction to.

"The Fool is the protagonist in the story the rest of the cards spell out. The dog represents his animal instincts, and cliffs...well," he paused. "Cliffs can be many things. Adventure, insanity, love." He drummed the table slowly with his square fingertips. "At any rate, he's heading into the unknown."

Jolie stared at the card for several moments after he'd stopped talking, pleased with the small story- or start of one-told in images on the card. She smiled.

"I like it," she said, then blushed at her inarticulateness. She was afraid it spoke volumes.

"The Major Arcana contains powerful archetypes, figures we all recognize, part of the collective unconscious. These are the characters that appear in the myths and stories of all peoples. You've seen the Fool before, he's the youngest brother in the fairy tales. You know the one I'm talking about? The two older brothers head out first, looking for gold, or the princess or the keys to the kingdom. But they blow it by being dicks to some sorceress or elf or whatever. Then the youngest brother heads out, all naive and full of heart. He gives his lunch to the old beggar woman by the roadside. He stops and helps the squirrel gather his acorns. He does something, in his well-intentioned innocence, that the magical elements are attracted to and wish to reward. Something an older, more experienced person might think was useless, a waste of time. And he gets the gold, or the princess, or the keys to the kingdom."

Jolie nodded, then, after a moment, when it seemed he wouldn't continue, offered a hesitant smile.

"I want to thank you for getting me this job. Can I cook you dinner, tomorrow?"

He grinned, handing her the notebook and marker he'd used earlier.

"That'd be lovely. Write down your address for me. I have a terrible sense of direction, but I'll give myself plenty of time."

Holding the notebook so he couldn't see what she was doing, she drew a buried treasure sort of map that led to her apartment. She handed it to him and his face lit up.

"Aye matey! I've always dreamed of being a pirate! This'll lead me old peg-legs right to ya," he spoke in a piratical voice, leering theatrically.

She stood, pleased he'd liked the map so much.

"Great. Come around 6?"

He nodded, his large brown eyes twinkling.

"Lookin' forward to it."

§

At 6 am Jolie's alarm rescued her from the dream. Gasping, she sat up in bed, the vision swiftly receding.

Again, she'd walked through the forest and sat on the dock that jutted over the lake. Legs kicking slowly over the still surface, she gazed at the statue across the way. Surrounded by overgrown roses, the figure of a woman peered at Jolie over her left shoulder. Seemingly unclothed, although the roses were too tall to say for sure, Jolie could see enough of her back to make out the large, tear shaped hollow in it, dark with shadows. The sight is so diverting she doesn't notice the storm rolling in until she hears the thunder. The dock pitches wildly as she jumps to her feet; no matter how many times she has the dream, it always comes as a surprise that the dock has somehow broken free of its mooring. As the world goes dark she decides to take her chances and swim for shore, but when she looks the shores have disappeared, and even when lightning strikes she can't see them. The white fork of light touches the water close to her, making the waves crackle with electricity, the boom of thunder shifting into the sounds of her alarm as she is yanked from one world to the next.

Once her heart slowed down she headed to the kitchen, turning on the kettle. Outside the world looked forbidding; thick, dark clouds lay heavily upon the tops of the trees. Hurrying back to the bedroom, she layered herself in the clothes she'd set out the night before. Thunder whip-cracked through the air, rattling the old windows and making her jump. Jolie and her cat, Boots, stared at each other, alarmed.

"Boots!" she said, picking up the cat from the end of her bed. "Tell me I'm being silly. It was just a dream. And this is just a storm." She stroked the smooth fur between the cat's ears. "Right?"

Boots had shown up not long after the dreams had started. Jolie had returned from work to find her sitting on the fire escape outside of her kitchen; the cat hadn't hesitated when offered cream, then tuna. She was back the next day and on the third day moved in. The apartment building was a once-grand home that had been divided into eight units and pets weren't allowed. Jolie couldn't afford the fine they would impose on her if Boots was found, but she also couldn't afford being alone. Jolie had been glad when the cat took to sleeping with her. Waking up to the presence of another creature made it almost bearable. Although she was not an overly affectionate animal, her huge golden eyes seemed to understand more than most humans.

Boots squirmed to be let down, then stalked back to the foot of the bed and curled back into a ball with deliberation. She stared at Jolie, daring her to try it again. Jolie laughed once, but it came out sounding flat. Pulling her socks on, she returned to the kitchen to turn off the kettle.

§

An hour later she stood outside of an old Victorian house. There was no sign out front, she looked again at the paper Jamie had written the address on, now rain splattered. The street number matched, but she continued to stand on the sidewalk, hunched under her red umbrella, staring up at the decaying wreck. The neighborhood had several old Victorian homes, along with newer houses, but this was certainly the worst looking of the bunch. At a glance it looked gray, but this was merely the weathered wood showing through the last vestiges of an ancient paint job. On the wide front porch, a wicker couch and chairs rotted out their final years. She might have walked away, assuming it was the wrong place, but for the smell of vanilla wafting out the screen door. Her stomach grumbled audibly as she rang the bell.

For a moment she heard nothing inside, but when she looked down she saw a calico cat staring at her, yellow eyes wide and curious.

"Hey, beautiful," Jolie said, crouching down to let the cat smell her fingers through the screen. The calico sniffed delicately, blinked at her, then walked away. A moment later Jolie heard footsteps.

The woman she'd seen in the book store opened the inner door all the way.

"Jolie!" she said, and her eyes were bright with curiosity. "I'm Greta, come in, let's talk in the kitchen."

Greta walked quickly down the dark hallway toward the back of the house; her pale hair, piled on top of her head in a loose bun, was like a beacon in the dimness. Jolie followed, taking in the cracked plaster walls, the empty echo of their footsteps.

"Do you have any experience?" Greta asked, glancing at Jolie as they entered the kitchen. Unlike the rooms they'd passed, the kitchen seemed updated.

Jolie nodded. "Not professional experience. But I used to cook and bake all the time."

Greta pulled several loaves of bread out of the convection oven and slid them onto a metal rolling rack to cool.

"It's not hard. Just follow the recipes, you'll do fine," Greta glanced at her. "Jamie said you were just what we needed."

"Does he work here too?" Jolie asked, confused.

Greta opened her mouth, then closed it again, smiled. "No. I wouldn't have anything to sell if he worked here. So," Greta tied an apron on and handed one to Jolie, "find the place ok?"

"Yeah. You don't have a sign up, though. No walk-in business?"

Greta shook her head. "None. In fact, if anyone knocks don't answer. We take orders on the phone and I do deliveries in the afternoon. Most places just have standard orders, so there aren't that many calls." Greta paused. "Actually, if anyone does call, I'd like you to answer it. Take an order. Place, date, quantity. If they ask for me, say I'm on a delivery and I'll call them back. Ok?"

"Sure," Jolie said.

"I just don't like being interrupted; might end up burning something. A couple of our customers act like they get paid by the spoken word. The guy who does the ordering for the downtown market and also the guy over at Chanelles. Have to practically hang up on them!" Jolie was following her into the pantry,

Greta's perfectly round back side swaying under a snug orange sweater skirt. The black glittery tights vied for attention, but were no match. Jolie thought she knew why these guys didn't want to let Greta off the phone.

The pantry was just big enough for them both to stand in. Greta grinned, as though she had heard Jolie's thought.

"Yeah, guys aren't that hard to figure out. Generally."

Jolie wanted to ask if Jamie was the exception, but she had no idea what their relationship might be. She supposed she ought to try to get some sense of that before he came by her apartment later.

"It was really nice of Jamie to ask you about this job for me," she said, after being shown where everything lived in the pantry. "Have you known him a long time?"

Greta shook her head. "I met him shortly after I got to town, about eight months ago. I was going to Illuminations a lot. He pretty much haunts the place."

"Bella gave me the impression he lives there," she said, hoping she wasn't coming off as too nosy.

"Yeah, he's got nowhere to go. His family disowned him, and he's got nothing. He's been living hard a long time. Not too many places are going to hire him. Now, let me show you how the mixer works."

Jolie refrained from asking any more questions during the rest of the kitchen tour. Afterward, Greta had her make a batch of chocolate cookies, which she deemed good, then told her they could call it a day.

"Tomorrow will be busier, I don't want to overwhelm you right off the bat."

Jolie shrugged. She'd enjoyed the last hour of baking. Greta had put on some poppy German band and the time had flown by, with Greta occasionally singing along or doing a couple dance steps. Jolie didn't get the sense this was done for her benefit, but if she caught her looking Greta would smile at her, half inviting, half teasing.

"Oh!" Greta said, as Jolie was buttoning her sweater to leave. "Where do you live?"

"Cherry. By Boulevard."

"You know, there's a path through the woods," and she pointed behind her, at the back door. "It runs right behind that block. It'll take you half the time."

Jolie grinned. "Really? I could commute through the forest?" she asked.

Greta made a face. "I want to live in a world where the word *commute* doesn't even exist!"

Jolie laughed aloud, pleased, somehow, by the other woman's annoyance that the world that was not as beautiful and exciting as it should be.

"I'll try it now, then." Jolie said.

Greta grinned, approving. "The path doesn't really split," she said, opening the back door and handing Jolie her umbrella. "Just keep walking. See you tomorrow."

§

Fall's approach had become visible on the trees outside her apartment these last few days, but in the slick dimness of the forest the palette subdued to moss and shadow. Jolie walked hurriedly under her umbrella, stopping only when she reached the lake to orient herself. It was an oval shaped body of water; she stood at one narrow end, the cottage she had mentioned to Jamie several hundred yards to her left, its stone walls and pitched roof tucked right into the trees. The path continued around the opposite side of the lake, towards home.

It was lighter here, out from under the trees, and she paused for a minute to take in the view. The bark on the trees was black and soft with rain, the cottage across the way a rustic bastion of solitude. Rain pin-cushioned the surface of the water, each drop causing a small shimmering splash. Her boots were starting to leak, and the hand that held the umbrella was chilled through, but for the duration of a breath her heart swelled with the scene before her.

Then she noticed the figure.

Near the cottage a woman in a long, hooded rain poncho stood, staring right at her. With her bright red umbrella, Jolie supposed she'd be hard to miss.

As though moving in slow motion, her left hand rose and offered the woman her open palm. Not a wave so much as an acknowledgment. Across the water, the figure responded in kind. She was far enough away that Jolie couldn't be sure, but she thought the face cracked into a smile before the woman turned and disappeared into the trees behind her. Jolie didn't think there was a trail on that side of the lake; she wondered where the woman was going and why she didn't duck into the empty cottage. If she'd been that close to shelter, she would have taken it in this weather. Shivering as the rain pelted harder, she turned and hurried home.

§

Jamie frowned with concentration as he flipped through the deck, pulled out the card.

"The Magician is the next card in the deck, the second card in the Major Arcana."

He had arrived an hour ago, only a little late, carrying a fistful of mums plucked from a garden along the way. She had found a jar for these, then served up the pasta with homemade sauce, a few drops of which had splashed on her arm. This had sent him crashing through her freezer for ice, wrapping ice cubes in a T shirt he pulled from his pack, then gently dabbing her barely scalded arm. She didn't know whether to be flattered or annoyed.

Over dinner he had told her about living in a redwood tree in California, eating out of the dumpster of a nearby cereal factory where he had briefly worked and where it was possible to get high on the amount of sugar in the air.

He was quick to mention that he'd been a junkie. She had the impression he always told people this early on, that it was an important part of his personal mythology. And with a habit as long lived as his, how could it not be? Ten years in the arms of Sister Morphine was how he referred to it, and she thought she read more nostalgia than regret in his face.

From this topic he had grown morose. A friend of his had recently died of an overdose. After an awkward stretch of silence, she'd asked if he had his cards with him, if he'd tell her about the next one.

Surely, he'd said, and cleared both their plates before pulling the cards from his back pack. They were wrapped in an old bit of silk cloth which he draped over her plastic kitchen table. On the card, a man in a long white robe held one arm skyward, wand in hand. The other hand pointed towards the ground. To his right stood a table with a cup, a pentacle, a sword, a wand. Flowers surrounded the scene.

"The Magician," Jamie said. "Remember the Fool's hobo stick, with the bag hanging over his shoulder?"

Jolie nodded.

"That's also a wand. But while the Fool doesn't know the power he possesses, the Magician is in control of his. The stuff on the table represents earth, air, fire, and water. All are at his disposal." He leaned back, his face breaking into a wide grin at something outside the kitchen window. "Look, it's a full moon!" he said, pointing to the clearing sky.

She glanced at the window, taking in the sudden brightness of the outside world.

"I don't suppose you'd want to walk in the woods?" she asked.

His eyes lit up and he nodded, grinning.

"Fairy child," he said, standing and making a sweeping gesture towards the door, "lead the way."

§

"You're mooning over the moon," she said. They stood outside, looking at the swollen silver orb above the trees.

He turned to her, a huge smile on his face, his eyes glistening.

"I can't help it. It's singing to me."

She followed his gaze, tried to let the sight fill her up the way it seemed to fill him. Her ability to feel the beauty before her did not seem to match his.

"I want to see things the way you see them," she said. He said nothing and she felt, after a moment, embarrassed by the admission. "Come on, it'll be even prettier over the lake."

The trees swallowed them. The leaves, in the moonlight, waved at them like black, papery hands.

"This is an old forest," Jamie said. "Look how tall these trees are."

Jolie craned her neck back to take in the height of them, then returned her gaze to the path, watching for rocks and tree roots.

"I think these woods are the reason I took this apartment," she said. "I was driving down the road and saw the rental sign. I looked right past the building and saw these trees. They reminded me of the woods around my parents' house, before the developer bought the land and tore them all down. I miss those woods."

"Aww, no! They tore down your woods?"

His indignation made her smile.

"I think that's what made my mom give up, stop trying to get better. She loved those woods, and they tore down everything beyond the two acres our house was on. And once she died my father sold our house to the same developer, gave me a couple grand, and headed out to California with his new girlfriend. On our last night in the house I snuck out and filled the bulldozers' gas tanks with sugar. I was so angry; I didn't care if I got arrested. Our home was wonderful, over 200 years old, with gardens that had taken generations to grow. My parents had met hiking in those woods. And they were going to bulldoze it to build a half dozen McMansions. The bulldozers didn't run the next day, but I know that later, after I moved here, they tore the place down."

Jolie was breathing quickly, the words having poured out of her like a dam breaking. Jamie gently grabbed her arm. She stopped walking, allowed him to wrap his arms around her.

"I'm sure your mama'd be proud of you. You're a fighter."

He held her close and she hid her face in his chest, her tears dampening his shirt until, reluctantly, she pulled away.

"Let's keep walking," she said, voice hoarse.

They reached the lake a few minutes later.

Moonlight silvered the surface as she led him to a fallen tree by the water's edge where she often sat. The air was cool and moist, it seemed natural to sit close for warmth. They looked out at the lake in quiet intimacy for a moment, the last insects of summer strumming the air around them. The scent of tobacco and scented oil coming from Jamie was strangely comforting.

"Jamie, how do you know Greta?"

He picked up a rock from the forest floor, tried to skip it across the water. It sank.

"She's a customer of mine; came in enough that we've gotten to know one another."

Jolie nodded.

"Did I ask you how the bakery was?" he asked. "This old brain has some holes in it."

She scoffed. "You can't be much past thirty!" He said nothing, and she assumed she was right. "It was kind of fun. I've never met anyone like Greta. She seems so comfortable being herself."

Jamie nodded, but slowly, as though trying to decide if he really agreed. "Greta's a complicated girl."

"She's really beautiful," Jolie said, watching his face carefully out of the corner of her eye.

He shrugged. "We share a lot of interests, unusual ones that have caused us to become friends quickly. I like Greta, but she's really damaged." He held her eye as he said it. Jolie blushed, looked out across the water. He'd known what she was really asking.

"Over that way is the little cottage I was telling you about the other day. Can you see it?"

He leaned forward. "I think so! Now that you say it. Just barely. Can kinda see the darker shape of the roof line. That's amazing-how have I missed that?"

"Ever since I saw it I've wanted to go over there. I've tried walking off the trail in that direction, but the brambles get thick and thorny. Still, I guess it's reachable. I saw someone walking over that way as I was coming back from the bakery this morning."

"You took this trail back from Greta's?"

"Yeah. She told me about it as I was leaving today. Said it would take half the time."

She was about to tell him about the cookies she'd made when they heard a distant creak, followed quickly by a thud. They stopped talking, staring in the direction of the cottage.

"What was that?" Jolie whispered. Jamie shook his head, peering into the darkness. Across the lake they saw a light travel along the windows of the cottage. A sickly green light, there one moment, gone the next. Then the creak and bang again, such as an old door with rusted hinges might make as it opened and slammed shut.

They sat completely still, listening. Finally, Jamie turned to her, grabbed her hand.

"Maybe that was nothing. But I've got a feeling like we ought to get out of here."

"Me too," she whispered. The bugs had all gone silent, but she chose not to point it out. Hand in hand they tip-toed back to civilization.

§

Jamie left shortly after they returned to her apartment. He gave her a long hug and suggested they hang out night after next. She'd offered to make him coffee, taken off guard by his sudden need to leave. Her surprise must have shown. He explained that he needed to make a phone call, but when she offered him her phone he shook his head, saying it would be a long talk.

After he told her this she offered a terse goodbye, then huffed off to the kitchen and started angrily washing dishes. A part of her was ashamed of herself even in the moment, but she couldn't stop, couldn't find it in her to act differently. Who would he be calling but another woman?

The next morning she schooled her face before walking into Greta's kitchen, offering a polite smile to her new boss as she hung up her coat by the door and tied on an apron. Greta wore a pink vintage tutu over black leggings and looked completely adorable.

"You look tired," Greta said, offering her a smile. "Fun night?"

"Not particularly," Jolie said, turning away quickly.

"Well, we can make coffee if you want. Today we're doing four dozen heart shaped maple cookies for a bridal shower on top of the usual orders, so I'm going to have you start on those."

Greta got her the recipe, pans, and cookie cutters she would need, threw a few loaves of bread in the oven, and left the kitchen. Jolie could hear her footsteps heading upstairs when the phone rang.

"Hello, you've reached Gingerbread."

The manager at the local market asked for a half dozen extra loafs of pumpernickel, and Jolie said she thought that'd be fine, she'd have Greta call him if there was a problem.

For the next hour she rolled out and cut cookies, taking Greta's loaves out of the oven when the timer went off. When Greta walked in the back door Jolie jumped.

"I thought you were upstairs!" she said.

Greta smiled, shook her head. "Sorry, I had to run out. Thanks for taking out the bread. I'll be back down in a minute, I just need to change."

Jolie nodded and began putting her trays in the oven. As she put the last one in the phone rang.

"Hello, thanks for calling Gingerbread." She waited, hearing nothing. "Hello, Gingerbread?" she tried again. And then she heard it. Breathing. It wasn't heavy breathing, but there was a slight whistle on the exhalation. "I think you have a bad connection," she offered, before hanging the phone up.

Greta came back in as she was replacing the phone, dressed in black pants and a kimono style top.

"Who was that?"

"Chanelle's," Jolie lied. "They want an extra half dozen loaves of pumpernickel."

Greta nodded, and Jolie didn't think she imagined the look of relief on her face.

At eleven they took a break. Jolie made some coffee and sat down on the back porch with a plateful of cookies, smiling despite herself at the decadent lunch. Afterward she found the bathroom, a little room close to the front door with visible pipes running up the wall and along the ceiling. As she was washing her hands she glanced down at the wastebasket and noticed the wrappers for a dozen Band-Aids, at least.

"What'd she do?" she whispered to her reflection which looked, at any rate, perkier than it had that morning.

In the hallway she stopped to admire a small charcoal sketch framed on the wall, a dreamy depiction of a house made by several trees leaning into one another and winding their branches together. It reminded her of Arthur Rackham's illustrations, in the story book her mother loved to read to her from when Jolie was a girl. With surprise she realized the work was signed. By Greta.

After lunch Greta hung around and made apple scones while Jolie decorated cookies. Greta had music playing, and conversation didn't feel necessary, but after a bit the caffeine kicked in. Feeling better, Jolie asked Greta where she had grown up.

"I was born in Deutschland, yah?" she said, with an over-the-top German accent, cutting the dough to weigh on a kitchen scale. "Dad was military, there used to be a lot of American armed forces over there. My parents sent me to German babysitters and German daycare for years before I learned the language. I still remember how terrifying that was, not being able to understand anything. I moved back to the states when I was ten and stayed with my mom's sister and her family. Had just as much culture shock there as in daycare," Greta shook her head, a rueful grin on her face.

"Are you glad now, though, that you were exposed to so much?" Jolie asked, glancing up from the glazing job she was doing. "I was home schooled until the last two years of high school. I really wish I'd seen more, met more people. Not to mention, my mom didn't do the best job teaching math, as it turned out."

"You're from around here then?" Greta asked.

"A couple hours north. I came here a few months ago, sort of on a whim. I wanted to go somewhere totally unfamiliar." She glanced up to find Greta looking at her with a shrewd expression.

"Something bad happen?" she asked.

"My mom died. And my dad's girlfriend made it clear that he needs me out of his life, so he can recover. I think she's just uncomfortable with the fact that we're so much closer in age than they are. And that they were probably seeing each other while my mom was still alive."

"Bitch," Greta hissed, but a smile tugged the corners of her lips. "Well, we can start a little orphan bakers club, anyway. My whole family died in a plane crash. That's why I ended up with my aunt in the states."

"Jesus!" Jolie cried. "What happened?"

"We were going on vacation-"

"You were on the plane too?"

Greta nodded, oiling her pans.

"We were headed to Istanbul. My mother wanted to see the street markets, the architecture. Mostly, I think, she wanted to shop somewhere there wasn't two feet of snow on the ground. It was winter and freezing. The plane we took was a little puddle jumper, and we were all bundled up because we had to board on the runway. My brother was seven, he looked like a blue marshmallow in his snow suit.

I never found out where we crashed. There are so many little countries between Germany and Istanbul. Hungary, Romania, Austria, Bulgaria." Greta stared at the oiled pan as she placed the scones on it, as though it were reflecting the scene back up at her. "We hit a blizzard, and the pilot tried to land us in a clearing at the top of a mountain. But he botched it and we crashed. Almost everyone was killed on contact."

"How do you not know where... I mean... someone found you..." Jolie's question trailed off. There was not a thing to say, she realized, that seemed appropriate.

"My brother Hank and I were the only ones who survived. He froze to death three days later. Eventually I was found by a group of cross-country skiers, but no one ever found the plane. Oddly enough, though, they found Hank the next spring. His skeleton, anyway. There are still wolves in that part of the world. They said that was probably what got to him."

Jolie could not find words for the shocking tale. Setting down the glaze brush that dangled limply from her hand, she went over and hugged Greta.

"Might be time for me to stop feeling sorry for myself," she said, as she let her arms fall back to her sides. Greta had returned the hug, but quickly busied herself the moment Jolie ended it.

"Definitely time for brighter topics today," Greta said, putting the pans in the oven. "Like Halloween!"

Jolie smiled as she carried all her utensils over to the sink to begin washing up. "Your favorite holiday?"

Greta smiled widely as she set the timer. "No contest."

§

Jolie's shift ended a little after two. Greta paid her in cash and sent her home with a loaf of bread. On the way out the back door Jolie almost stepped on a plate with two cookies, sitting by the stairs on the back porch.

"You want me to bring this in?" she asked Greta through the door, but the blond woman shook her head.

"An offering to the fairies!" she said, then giggled, her blue eyes twinkling mischievously. Jolie had no idea if she were kidding or not, but it didn't matter. Greta was delightfully odd, she decided, and with good reason.

After a two hour nap she awoke rested, but anxious. At work she had been too tired, and then too distracted by Greta's strange tale, to think much about Jamie. But now there was nothing stopping her, and her heart beat out a clear instruction: go find him. She knew it was a flimsy pretext, but grabbing the cash Greta had given her, she headed to Illuminations to do some shopping.

Rips in the clouds showed blue sky as she walked downtown. Bella was talking to an older man as she walked in, and she offered Jolie a tight half smile. Jolie gave a quick wave, then made her way to a display of Tarot decks and began reading over the packages. There were beautiful, quirky, and interesting decks, but eventually she found herself drawn back to the same one Jamie had, the Rider-Waite deck in its iconic yellow case.

"Maybe you should talk to the police if you're

that concerned!" Bella hissed at the man she'd been having the hushed conversation with. Jolie looked up, surprised. The man looked pointedly at her, clearly telling her to butt out. His eyes were deep set in his long, narrow face, his hair prematurely white.

"I think I've answered all your questions," Bella added, nodding towards the door.

Lips tight, the man tilted his hat to Bella then walked past Jolie and out the door.

Bella's chest was heaving as she caught Jolie's gaze. "You know," she said, "we get some real fruit balls in here."

Jolie made a sympathetic face, not knowing what to say.

"Sorry, hon, didn't mean to put you in the middle of it," Bella said, putting a smile on her face. "You need any help with the decks there?"

Jolie handed her the deck she wanted, then asked if Jamie was around, saying there was a book he'd recommended she read about Tarot, and she couldn't remember the name.

"I think he's up there, though sometimes he leaves out the back, so no telling."

Upstairs the door was closed but the sign wasn't up, so she knocked.

"Jolie!" Jamie cried, opening the door and

looking like there was no one he'd rather see. "What are you doing here?"

"Buying a tarot deck," she said, cautious, not wanting to show how glad she was to see him.

He ushered her in. The little table he did readings on was covered in books. An open notebook lay on top, revealing a geometrical sketch. He snapped it shut, pushing it into his bag with one hand while the other pulled a book out of a stack leaning against a wall.

"Well then you must get this book to explain the cards," he said, handing her a thick, purple, paperback volume. She flipped through the pages as though she were reading.

"Are we still on for tomorrow night?" he asked. Jolie sensed he was asking more with this question.

"I don't know, did you still want to meet up?" she asked, not looking up from the book.

Jamie reached out and took it out of her hand. Looking up she saw him frowning at her.

"I like you, Jolie. And while it might not look like I've got anything to do but hang out in this bookstore, I've got some pots boiling, some projects that I can't leave alone too long. As we get to know each other, maybe I'll tell you about them. Can you live with that?"

Her cheeks were burning. Was she really so transparent? She nodded once, not altogether satisfied. "I just thought, last night, it sounded like you had to leave to call another woman. Your girlfriend?"

He shook his head. "I did need to leave to call a woman, but she's not my girlfriend, and it wasn't like that. Just a friend I'd promised to help with something."

"Greta?" she asked, then wished she hadn't.

His eyes narrowed. "I don't play twenty questions, Jolie."

"Forget I asked," she said, looking down at the book in her hand. "Tell me about the next card?"

He reached out and squeezed her hand, then grabbed his deck.

"The High Priestess, one of my favorites; card of mystery, subconscious, intuition."

He pulled the card out, handed it to her.

A woman sat between two pillars, one white, one black. She wore a flowing blue robe and a crown that looked like a full moon set between two curving white horns. A veil hung behind her, draped between the two pillars. The fabric, decorated with pomegranates, did not quite block the view of the large body of water that lay beyond.

Jamie moved to sit next to her on the couch,

his arm resting along the cushion behind her. He was so close she found his words hard to hear over the blood hammering in her ears.

"The High Priestess's world is hidden behind the veil. The deep, dark places of the mind are hers. That body of water behind her is bigger than you see on almost any of the cards. Could be deep as the ocean, and all sorts of things could lie beneath it." The bitter smell of his hand-rolled cigarettes breathed out from his skin. "There are some ties to the tale of Persephone here: the pomegranates, the crown. You know the story?"

Jolie shook her head.

"One of the Greek myths. Persephone's mother is Demeter, Mother Nature. One day, mom goes out to make the grains grow and the trees fruit, and Hades, the god of the underworld, rides up in his black carriage and steals Persephone. She cries and mourns the loss of sunlight and fruits, refuses to be happy with any of the jeweled wonders of his world.

"In the end her mother rescues her, but just before she does Persephone breaks down and eats six pomegranate seeds Hades offers her. She'd gone months without eating anything, knowing that once she did she wouldn't be able to leave. The six pomegranate seeds confine her to spending six months of the year in the underworld, for eternity."

"A jeweled underworld," she said.

"Doesn't sound too bad, does it?" he asked. She shook her head, saw him become distracted. "You got the time?"

She glanced down at her watch. "Almost six."

"I got a client coming, going to have to say goodnight."

Reluctantly, she stood. "Goodnight then."

Standing, Jamie pulled her to him and kissed her, taking her by surprise. His arms wrapped around her, one hand cupping the back of her head. Too soon he pulled away, opened the door for her.

"See you tomorrow, Jolie."

Downstairs she bought the book and the deck, then wandered out into the twilight. The sky was a bewitching shade of purple, and she walked slowly, looking up. Halfway down the block she crossed the street and saw the man who'd been speaking to Bella, sitting in his car, staring intently towards the store. She glanced over her shoulder once she was past him, just in time to see Greta opening the door to Illuminations, the wind scattering her loose blond hair across the back of her black dress.

§

That night the dream was different. Again, she

sat on the dock, legs dangling in the water, only this time she watched from a distance as though she were someone else. She watched the dock spring loose from its moorings then float across the darkening lake towards the grassy knoll on which she stood. Lightning flashed and electrified the water. A dark-haired girl, hunkered low on the raft and trying not to fall in, was too distracted to see what the lightning illuminated. But up on the knoll, she saw. Beneath the surface was a whole other world. Where the sandy lake bottom should have been, a purple sky stretched on forever above the upside-down trees, whose roots seemed to snake, invisibly, into the air of our world.

§

Jamie came over after dark, greeting her with a kiss.

"I've been looking forward to this all day," he said.

"Me too," she said, then looked away, embarrassed. Her limited dating experience had not included bare declarations of this sort. He set down his pack and pulled out a bottle of wine.

"I don't think I have a cork screw," she said, dismayed. She had the next day off, and the wine seemed like a dark red ribbon the night could travel along, winding through conversations and declarations, finally spooling in her bed.

"Me trusty knife'll do the job," he said, the pirate voice back. He winked at her as he began gouging out large chunks of cork. She bit her lip, worried he might slice his fingers. Eventually he got it, or most of it. They filtered the wine through a paper towel to get the tiny bits of remaining cork out before they toasted each other.

"To intriguing strangers," Jamie said, clicking his mug against hers.

He had an Indian blanket strapped onto his pack, and he led her out on the fire escape, unrolling it there so the narrow metal walkway was comfortable enough to sit on. They sat cross legged, knees touching.

"This is my favorite season," Jamie said, with a contented sigh. "The leaves turning glorious, then withering. Makes me think of that Poe story, the Mask of the Red Death. Know it?"

She nodded, swirling her cup so the moonlight rippled through her wine. "There's a masked ball," she said. "Everyone attends, trying to forget the plague that is going to kill them. In the end, they all die."

He grinned. "That's what this is. Autumn: the great masked ball, the fiery pageant before winter claims nature and her subjects in its deadly grip."

She laughed, surprised. "I'm going to think about that every fall now."

"And right in the middle of the season, Halloween, when death enters the party."

"Is that your favorite holiday, too?" she asked, Greta suddenly on her mind, intruding.

"Definitely," he said, reaching into his sweatshirt pocket for a pouch of tobacco. "Samhain is the other name for it. There's so much legend, mythology, folklore about it. Remember what I was telling you about the Persephone myth the other day?"

She nodded, sipped her wine. The drink made her mouth feel dry and prickly.

"Six months in her mother's world, and six below with Hades. Well, every culture has a story to explain the change of power between spring and summer, fall and winter. In faerie folklore it's said that there is a light court and a dark court, the Seelie and the Unseelie. On Samhain the Unseelie faeries take power for the next six months." He opened his mouth as if to say more, then grinned. "I particularly like that explanation."

"Greta was talking about faeries the other day. She left a plate of cookie on the back porch for them." Jolie glanced at him out of the corner of her eye. "She's real excited about Halloween too."

His lips pressed together for a moment.

"I'm not supposed to talk about Greta's business," he said, speaking slowly. "She had something extraordinary happen to her, once. She's hoping it might happen again." He finished rolling his cigarette, lit it. "We should talk about something else. She's my best customer, she pays for my discretion. Maybe she will open up to you, once she gets to know you better."

"You read her cards, right? I mean, I'm just confused; is that usually a confidential thing?"

He shook his head. "She's paying me to help her with something else." He paused, sipped his wine. "You look really beautiful tonight, by the way."

She'd taken pains with her hair and makeup, and traded her usual baggy clothes for a fitted top and snug jeans.

"Thanks," she said, a bashful grin stealing over her face as she took in the wide-eyed admiration on his. She decided, taking in this look, that he wasn't merely trying to change the subject.

Leaning over he placed his lips against hers, their mouths opening, tongues tasting like dirt and cherries from the wine. When she was on his lap she realized that, skinny as she was, he was skinnier still. He wrapped the blanket around their shoulders and they went inside. In the bedroom, they undressed one at a time. Jamie whistled softly at her naked body then took off his own clothes, revealing a picture book's worth of illustrations tattooed across his chest, stomach and upper arms. They shivered as they kissed then hurried into bed, the cold having quickly gotten to them in their moment of distraction.

§

They slept late and woke to blue skies, the wind tugging gently on the leaves of the trees visible from her bedroom window. Jolie made them coffee, and they lounged in bed, made love again, and had breakfast at noon. Jolie wasn't ready for him to go when, after washing the plates for her, he said he had to read cards for someone. But she was ready to get outside, the beautiful day beckoning to her. After kissing him goodbye she headed towards the lake.

A ginkgo tree at the edge of the woods waved its golden fans at her; the maples were a full flaming red. Enough leaves had fallen that the trail was implied rather than visible. Squirrels were busy burying acorns, their bright black eyes glancing at her quickly before deciding she posed no threat.

Settling down against the log next to the lake she found she could hardly keep her eyes open. They had stayed up late and she wasn't accustomed to sharing a bed. The sun was a warm, golden poppy in the sky. She nodded off in minutes.

The dream seemed to begin immediately.

Again, she stood outside of herself, watching from across the lake. She saw herself sitting on the dock, the thin, serious girl; so lonely, so curious. It was not malice that made her cause the ropes that held the dock in place to untie. It was the will to set a sequence of events in motion, a desire to see where they would end. The roses beside her glowed in the storm light, the inch long thorns that guarded them slyly hidden by leaves. Their smell was intoxicating, she knew, but trapped in this stone body it had been a long time since she'd been able to breathe it in. She watched the dock stir loose and drift away from shore with a small thrill of anticipation.

§

Jolie awoke with a gasp. Disoriented and scared, she lurched to her feet, looking around as though expecting to find someone crouched behind a tree. She jogged back to the path, casting several backwards glances over her shoulder. She slowed down when her apartment was in sight, came to a standstill when she saw Jamie and Greta sitting on her fire escape.

Jolie reminded her feet to keep moving, told

her brain to put a cork in the bottle of paranoia that was trying to spill over all her thoughts at the sight of the two of them together. Jamie lifted his hand and waved, a cigarette burning between his fingers. She hurried up the stairs.

"What's going on?" she asked.

Greta seemed to sway slightly as she stood up.

"Sorry to intrude," she said. "Can we go inside?"

Jolie handed Greta the key, as she stood closest to the door, then gave Jamie a questioning look behind her back. His somber expression told her nothing.

"Mind if I close the blinds?" Greta asked once they were inside.

"Go ahead," Jolie said, sitting down on the couch, legs tucked under her. "As long as you're going to tell me what's going on."

When Greta had finished she perched on the edge of the couch. Jamie pulled a chair from the kitchen.

"Someone's looking for you?" Jolie guessed.

Greta bit her lip, nodded. "His name is Horace. He's an," Greta twirled a piece of hair around her finger, "an occultist, I guess you could call him. He'd say wizard, probably. Mysticism, esoteric beliefs, magick with a k; anything he thinks might bring him power. Mostly his knowledge just brings him a bunch of weak minded sycophants, some of whom happen to be wealthy." She paused, tugging her glittery tights up to her knee. The skin beneath, more visible as she tugged the fabric, was crisscrossed with small scratches. Boots stepped out from under the couch, stretched, and stalked out of the room.

"I might have helped myself to some of his ill earned money. Mostly just so I could get away from him." She sighed, closed her eyes. "He was in Illuminations yesterday, describing me to Bella. I didn't think she liked me much, but she lied for me, told him she hadn't run into anyone that matched my description."

"This guy, does he have white hair, very thin and intense looking?" Jolie asked.

Greta nodded, a laugh bursting forth suddenly from her lips. "He dyes it white!"

Jolie looked at Jamie. "Do you know him too?" she asked.

He shook his head. "Haven't had the pleasure."

"Um, don't take this the wrong way," she said to Greta, "but why come here?"

Greta leaned towards her. "Confidentially," she mock-whispered, "I think Jamie just wanted to see you."

"True," Jamie said, "But I also wanted to throw him off the trail if he was following us. He doesn't know what name she's going under, so as long as he doesn't see her go home he won't know where to look for her. She can cut home through the woods once it starts getting dark."

Jolie bit her lip.

"Greta? I was in Illuminations when he talked to Bella, and when I left the store I saw him in his car. He saw you go in there as they were closing."

Greta's eyes went wide, and then she laughed, a sickly laugh.

"Then he already knows where I live. He'd have waited and followed me home last night."

"What will he do if he finds you?" Jolie asked.

"Hard to say," she replied, her red Mary Janes tapping an anxious beat against the floor.

"If he knows where you live then why didn't he confront you last night?" Jamie asked, frowning. "Maybe he didn't follow you. He might've gone to take a piss and missed you leaving."

Greta shook her head, her face ashen.

"You don't know this guy. I lived in his house for several months; I've seen him go a week without sleeping, a month without eating once. Anything to get his brain sharp, or hallucinatory, or whatever state he thinks might help his magic. He has enormous self-control."

"Why did you stay there?" Jolie asked, hoping it wasn't a mean question, given the circumstances.

Greta shivered. "I thought he could help me find what I've spent my life looking for. But he couldn't, so I left to find it for myself."

"Did you..." Jolie stopped as footsteps were heard in the hallway. All three stared at the door until they heard the neighbors' key in the lock. Jolie exhaled, looked at the other two.

"Maybe you could get a security system put in?" she suggested to Greta.

Greta chewed her lip, staring off into space.

"I've thought about that," she said, finally. "But I suspect he could find a way past it."

"How...can he really do magic?" Jolie didn't manage to keep the skepticism out of her voice.

Greta shrugged. "Perhaps, but he wouldn't have to. He could pay someone to hack into the security network and find my pass code. Money works its own sorcery."

Jolie looked around her tiny apartment. She didn't really want extra company, but she was worried about Greta.

"You can sleep on the couch tonight, if you'd rather not go home," she offered.

Greta shook her head.

"Thanks. But I've got to get back to Strega. And I need to think things through. If he didn't bother me last night, he probably won't tonight."

"What do you think he's waiting for?" Jolie asked.

"For me to find what I'm looking for, so he can steal it from me."

Jolie sensed, somehow, that Greta was not ready to tell her what that was. The silence stretched out. Eventually, Jamie stood up.

"Let's get you home," he said to Greta. "I'll come back later."

"Knock three times, quickly, or I won't answer," Jolie said.

He nodded. "Mr. Wizard is going to get tired of this game, move onto something else before long. Rich people get bored real easy," he said. Greta looked unconvinced and Jolie said nothing, hoping he was right.

"Be safe," she said, locking the door behind them.

§

Jamie returned to the apartment an hour later

with nothing to report. He looked beat, and they went to sleep shortly after, Jolie only realizing how tense she'd been when Jamie curved his body around her, and her muscles began to melt. The next morning she woke before her alarm and dressed quietly, leaving him to sleep as she left for work.

The woods were damp and dim; the light which made its way through the layers of leaves was of a murky, underwater sort. She walked quietly, the stillness of the forest putting her on edge. Stopping to retie her boot she heard a murmuring sound. Crouching even lower, she tried to peer through the scrim of forest between the path and the lake. She froze as someone cleared their throat.

Shooting a glance behind her she saw no one. Raising herself up just slightly, she peered through a gap in the undergrowth. Twenty yards away Horace knelt by the lake with his back to her.

She was on slightly higher ground than him, and as she straightened up she found herself peering down on a strange tableau. He'd collected a small mound of rocks which he knelt in front of as he uttered a constant stream of harsh syllables, a guttural, monotone incantation that she could not make out a word of. His left hand held a dagger with which he stabbed the sandy lake soil over and over. She watched, hypnotized, the stab and slice of the knife pinning her in place, the fear turning her heart to ice.

The movement across the lake caught both of their attention. Something had moved in front of the cottage, and, seizing on the distraction, she quickly crept backwards, still crouched low. There was a bend in the path beyond which she did not think he'd be able to see her, and when she reached that she ran like mad. As she entered the yard of her apartment she stopped for breath. Looking at her watch, she saw she had just enough time to go to work the long way. Nerves jangling, she started in that direction, unprecedentedly glad for the early morning traffic.

§

Jolie found the backdoor locked and knocked three times, quickly, hoping Greta recalled what she'd said to Jamie the night before. Greta peeked around the curtain before unlocking the door and moving back to the mixing bowl. Her black pants and blue T shirt had batter splashed across them; she'd apparently forgotten an apron. She turned the mixer off and sat down on a tall stool next to the counter, looking Jolie over. Her eyes seemed barely open and she laughed, as though knowing what a wreck she must appear.

"Every time I started to drift off I heard some kind of creak in the house. Strega gave up trying to sleep with me after the fifth time I got up to check the closets and make sure the phone lines hadn't been cut."

Jolie hung up her purse, then leaned back against the door, which Greta had locked behind them.

"I saw him this morning. In the woods, near the cottage. I doubled back without him noticing and took the long route to work."

Greta looked considerably more awake at this news.

"What was he-thank god he didn't see you-the cottage?" As Greta's words tumbled out she slipped out of the stool, nearly falling backwards and catching herself on the counter.

"Were you involved with him..." Jolie hesitated, "...romantically?"

She'd caught Greta off guard. The blond woman looked near tears.

"Yes. Not for very long, though. We met at a New Age convention and he managed to draw my story out of me. And he actually believed me," Greta's voice cracked as she said this. She paused and took a deep breath before continuing. "No one had ever done that before, I'd always been alone with it. Not that I was eager to tell people, but I had tried. People I thought I could trust, who would know me well enough to know I wasn't lying. He believed me right away, said he could tell I wasn't lying, that he always knew when people were. I left the convention with him, moved into his huge old family home. He was a powerful lover and-this might sound twisted-a sort of father figure as well. I shared a lot with him before the first "gathering of acolytes." When they arrived, I saw they were all attractive, troubled young women he'd taken under wing, and all of them were giving me the stink eye. I thought the ceremony was pompous and artificial; I was a bit heartbroken, but I decided to leave the next day." Greta slouched back into the stool, her shoulders curving around her.

"He knew. His only real gift, I'm convinced, is being able to read people with incredible accuracy. The next morning, when I went to gather my things, I found my wallet gone. I had no money, no ID, no keys. He took all my shoes, and it was winter. He told me I would be starting as the lowest acolyte, and that this was part of the initiation. Like he wasn't scared of me leaving, like it was for my own good." Greta's voice was tight with anger. "It took me two months to steal the money, then con one of his little sycophants into giving me a ride to town."

"He must have really wanted this thing you are looking for," Jolie said, her voice careful. "Greta, I know you said he was the first person to believe you.

I'm guessing Jamie is the second. What if I promised to at least not disbelieve you?"

Greta had been staring at the floor, and now she glanced at Jolie with a wry smirk that somehow managed to drive home the ten-year age difference between the two women.

"Ok," she said, finally, as though humoring Jolie. "See if you can not disbelieve this: I went to another world as a child. Another realm, a parallel universe, whatever you want to call it. I want to return to it, Horace hopes to pull power from it, and Jamie wants to see it. Now," she said, standing and grabbing an apron, "Can we get to work? We still have to get today's order done."

Eyes wide, Jolie nodded.

§

Greta seemed incredibly preoccupied the rest of the day; it was a miracle only one batch of cookies was burnt. Finally, towards the end of the day, she turned to Jolie and asked if she would take her to the cottage sometime.

"You're not scared of running into Horace?" Jolie asked, laying aside her rolling pin for a moment. "What do you think he was doing there, anyway?"

"Looking," Greta sighed. "I'm terrified of running into him, but these woods..."

Jolie looked at her, eyebrows raised.

"Well, I've been a little obsessed with them, since I moved here. I would've sworn I'd walked every inch of them, and then you mention this cottage, that I've somehow never seen." She scraped another cookie onto a cooling rack. "It makes me wonder."

"Wonder what?" Jolie pressed.

Greta shrugged, as though at a loss to explain.

"Will you show it to me?" A note of pleading entered Greta's voice.

"Sure," Jolie relented. "Our next day off, I'll take you."

§

Jamie had stayed over every night, and on the morning she was to meet Greta she woke up next to him, took in the slow rise and fall of his back, and carefully crept from the room. She left a note on the counter saying she was running out for an hour and quietly shut the back door behind her. When she asked herself why she wasn't telling him about her and Greta's plans she came up with nothing concrete, just an image of him presenting the cottage to Greta with a flourish, as though he had conjured it up for her. The thought made her grit her teeth, her distaste at the thought of them together, or her cottage being shown in that way, like sand in her mouth.

Greta was waiting for her on the lawn behind her apartment, wearing tight green pants and a brown jacket, the brown wig half covered by a knitted, mustard colored cap. She smiled as Jolie approached.

"I brought cookies, in case you skipped breakfast," she said, holding out a huge snicker doodle.

"My favorite," Jolie said with a grin, tucking it in her pocket. "I don't think my stomach is awake just yet."

The women walked in silence, listening, turning to investigate the smallest noise. When they reached the lake, she pointed towards the cottage, entrenched in shadows.

Greta stared across the lake, her eyes wide, clearly seeing it for the first time.

"It's beautiful!" she said, the smile that broke over her face making Jolie glad it was just the two of them, somehow. "Let's go look inside!"

"We can try," Jolie said.

The women walked single file around the lake, trying to avoid the thorny vines and poison ivy, with only some luck. When they were fairly close to the lake they were stopped by a boulder in their path, and Greta stared at it as though it might turn into something else.

"I think we just need a good-sized tree branch

to stand on, and I could hoist myself to the top," Jolie said.

Greta soon found a broken branch that would gain them a foot, and together they dragged it over to the boulder. The branch was much heavier than it looked, and they were breathing hard by the end of it. Leaning against the boulder, Jolie looked at Greta.

"I believe you," she said. "I've always believed that kind of thing could happen. I think my mom did too, she always told me fairy tales like it was important for me to listen, not like she was trying to keep me busy, or put me to sleep, but like she had to teach me something."

Greta nodded, bit her lip. "Thank you," she said, finally, but Jolie could tell from the tone that Greta wasn't ready to tell her more. "Ready?" she asked, and Jolie nodded, hoisting herself up.

"Step carefully, the branch isn't real steady." Jolie waited at the top for Greta. Once up they scanned the woods around them.

"Over there is where I saw him," Jolie said, pointing.

Greta nodded, her attention quickly pulled back towards the cottage.

"We can check over there later, I can't wait to see this place!" She jumped, skidding as she hit the ground below, but staying on her feet. Jolie lowered herself down carefully, running a few steps to catch up.

Greta grinned at her as they made their way around the house, taking in the cottage slowly, as if savoring it.

"Now I'm hungry," Greta said, pulling another large snickerdoodle from her pocket.

"Ditto," Jolie said. She broke her cookie, putting half back in her pocket while she munched the other. The forest was always a quiet place, but the quiet around the cottage felt intentional, the kind of silence one might find in an empty cathedral. The walls, she realized, were covered in dark green lichen that made them look black at a distance. The windows were small, and cut into smaller squares by metal crosspieces. It was impossible to see anything in the darkness within. Staring at the window, Jolie's vision swam, and she leaned heavily against the wall. Behind her she heard Greta gasp.

"Horace, stop!" Greta cried out.

Jolie's world went dark.

§

For a long time there seemed to be blackness, then she and Jamie were sitting under a tree in a forest, surrounded by silent people dressed in shades of orange, red and gold. The people milled about, making graceful, quiet turns around the trees, their faces eyeless behind the masks they wore.

"This is the fourth card, the Empress," Jamie said, pointing to a woman who sat down on a rock between them. The woman smiled a cold smile. Her tiara was made of bones, and the necklace that glistened low on her chest was spider silk. She stared straight at Jolie, her eyes dark portals.

"The Empress is the card of Nature. She is passion, motherhood, life-" Jamie stopped mid-sentence as the figure raised her hand.

"Nature," the Empress said, and her voice was thick and sweet, the syllables swirling slowly on the air, collapsing into one another. "Nature is equally concerned with Death." She smiled again, and gestured around her at the autumnal figures.

One by one, they began to fall.

§

Jolie's eyes flew open, then immediately shut against the incredible headache.

"Aspirin!" she whispered. Jamie rose from her bedside, she heard him searching through the bathroom cabinet, his quick heavy footsteps returning moments later. Taking her hand, he uncurled her fist and placed two pills in it.

"Get you some water," he said, hurrying out

again. She put the pills in her mouth and chewed, gagging on their bitter taste but in too much pain to care. She chugged the glass when he returned and lay back down, her eyes still shut.

"What happened?" she asked.

He took her hand, squeezed it gently.

"I woke up and you were gone. I saw your note, but I'd kind of heard you leave and then fallen back asleep, and I knew it had been way more than an hour. Greta had told me you were showing her the cottage today, so I knew where to look. She was watching over you in case Horace came back, said he'd surprised you both, hit you on the back of the head before she could stop him. That goddamn..."

"How did she get away?"

Jamie exhaled heavily. "I don't know. I think she made some kind of bargain with him, but she won't tell me. I'm going to kill him, as soon as I think you're ok enough for me to leave the apartment. Do you want to go to the hospital?"

Jolie shook her head, squeezed Jamie's hand as if trying to read the lines of his palm with her fingers.

"Glad to wake up back home," she said, but even as she said it, even as sleep crept back in, she knew that this was not her home.

§

She slept most of the remainder of the day. Jamie stayed with her, reading to her and taking Greta's call when she phoned. She said Jolie should take a few days off but begged her to come in on Halloween and help her prepare the delivery for the festival. Half awake, Jolie merely nodded her assent.

The next morning she woke up feeling better. Jamie was fast asleep as she slipped into the bathroom, trying to see the back of her head with two mirrors. There was no discernible bump, and only a small scratch on the side of her face, which might have resulted from sliding down the side of the cottage.

She turned the shower on hot and got in, hoping the searing heat would help her remember the events of the day before more clearly. What would Horace have gained by knocking her unconscious? Nothing had been stolen from her. Presumably he didn't want a witness to whatever he was about to do to Greta, yet she somehow convinced him not to hurt her. Jolie turned the water off and toweled dry. Realizing her mouth tasted awful she squeezed some toothpaste onto her brush. She had just started brushing when it hit her. The cookie.

She quickly finished brushing and hurried out into the living room, looking for the coat she'd worn the day before. Her heart kicked against her chest as she looked over the living room and kitchen and didn't find it. In the bedroom, in a pile on the floor, she found it just as Jamie stirred.

Putting the coat on, she felt the shape of the cookie through the thin lining. She smiled at Jamie as he sat up in bed, wondering how much he knew.

"It's chilly this morning," she said, "but I'm starving! Want to walk to the market and get breakfast sandwiches?"

"Sure, baby," he said, giving her a sleepy-eyed smile. "I'm glad you're feeling better."

While he dressed she put the cookie in a tupperware container and pushed it to the back of a cabinet, not sure what she should do with it.

At the market, they bought steaming croissants filled with scrambled eggs, sausage, and cheese, then ambled over to the town square where the Halloween festival would take place in just three days.

Jamie carried their bag in one hand, his other arm wrapped around her shoulders. When she looked up at him he was smiling into the crisp blue sky, for all the world like he was happy, perhaps in love.

There were only a few scattered people dotting the town green when they arrived. Jamie took off his jacket and spread it out on the grass for them to sit on.

He chose a spot next to a flower bed full of orange and purple mums; they watched the bees, flying fast in the cool air, on their final pollen collection before the killing frost.

The croissant almost made Jolie swoon on the first bite. She devoured it in no time, then leaned back on her elbows.

"Tell me more about Halloween, Jamie," she said. "You said you like the folklore around it."

He lit a cigarette and lay on his side, facing her and the flowers.

"Halloween is when the veils between worlds are thinnest. Our world and the world of the dead, obviously, but other worlds as well. Throughout history there've been stories of people walking into other worlds, like parallel dimensions lined up next to ours. All over the world there are accounts of this happening, most of them older. People are so skeptical nowadays, brandishing their shield of science and using it to block out anything they don't understand. But maybe science and magic aren't mutually exclusive. Maybe, as I said, the 'faerie world" is a parallel dimension. I think people still walk into these other worlds, they just don't talk about it."

A cool breeze blew over them, she watched goose bumps pop up along his arm, but he didn't move. She'd long since noticed how he'd numbed himself to discomfort.

"You're hoping to go dance with faeries?" she asked, teasing.

He grinned broadly, blew a smoke ring. "I'd like nothing better. Except that you be there dancing with me," he smiled at her, and her heart pounded. She thought she might believe him.

"Magic has always fascinated me, it's a big part of why I fell in love with heroin the way I did. But drugs are false magic, just make you fall into a deep hole in your own world, so deep it feels like it might be somewhere else, for a while." His dark gaze had turned inward. Sitting up, he stubbed his cigarette out.

Jolie stood and offered him her hand. "Let's head over to Illuminations."

§

The store was less than a mile away and they walked hand in hand, faces tilted up to appreciate the sunlight that sieved through the red maples lining the sidewalks. People walked by them, on cell phones and in pairs, everyone seemingly out of sync with them, moving too fast, their voices snatched up by the wind and cast away. Jolie felt Jamie's hand, somewhat waxen in her own, and thought the two of them seemed like a thread separated from the weave of the human fabric.

"Jamie!" Bella said, when they finally walked in the door. She looked worried. "I need to talk to you. Alone," she added, apologetically.

"I'll browse upstairs," Jolie offered. Jamie nodded, following Bella into the small office, closing the door behind them.

Only two minutes later he reappeared, jaw set and eyes blazing.

"Let's go," he said.

"What is it?" she asked, but he shook his head, pulling her to her feet and rushing down the stairs.

"Thanks again, Bella," he said, with real feeling, and Jolie began to wonder if someone had died. Hurrying to keep up with him, she chased him halfway up the block before pulling him into an alley.

"What's going on? Where are we rushing to?"

Jamie looked around once, pulling the hood up on his sweatshirt although the sun was still out.

"Cops came around looking for me. I was on parole, out west, and I skipped out on it in order to get close to home, to a place I thought I might be able to stay clean. Well, somehow they knew to look for me at Illuminations. Someone tipped them off." His cheeks looked red with heat but the rest of him looked white, even his lips, which were pressed in a tight line of anger.

"What did you do?" she asked.

He rolled his eyes. "Breaking and entering, but it was fucking ridiculous. A bunch of us broke into a warehouse because it was raining and we had nowhere to go. While we were in there I overdosed. My so-called friends left me, the cops saw them fleeing and came in to investigate. They saved my life but charged me with a felony. The others had stolen a bunch of stuff, but clearly I hadn't taken anything."

Jolie put her hand on his arm, squeezed it in what she hoped was a reassuring way.

"Let's just get back home," she said.

§

At her apartment Jamie immediately got on the phone and started calling old friends, asking if the cops had come around looking for him, seeing if anyone had heard anything. After the first call, he unplugged the phone and took it into the bedroom, plugged it in there and shut the door. Jolie supposed he'd felt self-conscious speaking in front of her. His change in demeanor, once he was talking to his friend out west, was painfully transparent. He played a dumb, guffawing, down home version of himself, and she was reminded, oddly enough, of certain politicians. Even his accent changed for his audience.

She baked lasagna then cleaned the apartment as it cooked; scrubbing baseboards, sweeping beneath the old couch, cleaning things she'd never cleaned before. Her mind shut off and her hands did the thinking; thinking only about the task in front of them. When her brain tried to break through with a thought she shut it down, started cleaning faster. She wanted to be wrong about the cookie, she wanted to trust Jamie. She felt as she did in her dream, when she first realizes that the dock has drifted to the center of the lake. She was not quite ready to look up and greet the storm, if there was one to greet.

Finally, Jamie emerged from the bedroom, looking in better spirits.

"Any news?" Jolie asked.

Jamie shrugged. "Not really. It was good catching up with some people though. I'll give you some money towards the phone bill when it comes in."

She smiled, as if to say it didn't matter.

"I was thinking, you feel like getting us some wine?" Jolie asked. "I've got lasagna in the oven, and I thought we could just try to kick back and relax..."

His eyes had lit up at the word wine. "Sure, darling, I'll do that right now."

After dinner and wine Jamie leaned back, rolled a cigarette. "That was some good cooking. Just wished I'd thought to pick up a pie or something for dessert.

Jolie grinned. "You and your sweet tooth! I have a cookie, or half of one, that Greta gave me." She walked over to the cabinet, where she had put it in some tupperware. "You want it?"

"You want to split it?" he asked.

She shook her head. "I'm full."

He eagerly took the cookie, ate it without hesitation. Jolie watched, guilt rising in her at every bite. Why hadn't she just trusted him?

Knowing he wouldn't be awake long, she led him to the bedroom, took her shirt off as he kicked off his boots and laid back, his eyes barely open.

"I can't believe how sleepy I am, beautiful," Jamie said, "Or, most of me, anyway," he finished, with a glance towards the bulge in his jeans. He was smiling at her as his eyes closed.

"Jamie?" Putting her shirt back on, she walked over to him, perched on the edge of the bed.

"Jamie," she repeated, pinching his arm. When he did not respond she shook him, then slapped him across the face. Not so hard, but hard enough to wake someone.

He mumbled something incoherent and slept on, Greta's cookie winding through his blood stream, working its magic.

§

Jolie sat on the edge of the bed, feeling awful. Clearly, he hadn't known about the cookie. She wished she knew what was in it, what drug Greta had used. She hoped it wasn't something that would stir his longing for opiates. She pulled his boots off and threw an extra blanket over him, then rubbed his leg through the blanket as she sat, brooding. After several minutes, she realized she'd been staring at Jamie's pack on the floor.

A quiet voice in her head declared she was about to do something reprehensible, and after possibly poisoning him! But the voice wasn't loud enough; she wanted to know once and for all that she could trust him. He was a secretive person and she'd known him such a short time. Kneeling on the ground at the foot of the bed, she opened his pack and began taking things out, keeping track of their general order. A fantasy novel was on top, a cheap bottle of whiskey she'd known nothing about lay just below, almost empty. A tangle of dirty clothes came out in one clump. At the bottom of the sack lay his tarot deck and an old, cloth-bound hard-covered book. An Encyclopedia of Mythical Creatures. Sitting with her back against the bed, Jolie opened to the introduction and began reading. The author spoke of fairies being seen in different manifestations in different parts of the world, so that they would seem to be, if not real in the tangible sense, at least a part of the collective imagination. He went on to add that the fairy tales we are all familiar with often don't feature "fairies," as such, because it was considered bad luck to use their name. But what else were the witches, the kings and queens with magical powers, supposed to be? They were fairies, given another name for the safety of the story teller. Sitting close to her hearth on a dark winter evening, one eye on the rapt children's faces before her, and one on the small window behind them, the story teller would watch, anxious nothing should appear, bright eyes flashing with the strange knowledge of the other world, intrigued to hear itself spoken of. Saying their name could call them, and so the people of centuries past called them other things, and eventually these other things became characters in their own right.

Jolie finished the introduction and began flipping through the encyclopedia. Halfway through she nearly dropped the book.

The creature stared out from the page with cunning eyes. The Elle Maid, she read, and wondered at the redundant name, as she recalled elle meaning woman from high school French class. The beautiful fairy, it said, went to great pains to hide her hollow back, the clear give away to mortals that she was not one of them. She was known for stealing and eating small children, for living in the deepest parts of the woods where even the brave feared to go. In the dark months, she might venture to the edge of the forest and try to lure people to her. These people were never seen again. The few tales about her were Germanic in origin and were some of the oldest recorded, although they lacked the popularity that had favored some German fairy tales.

Jolie leaned back against the bed, heart pounding, thinking about how the woman in her dream displayed her hollow back as though purposely to Jolie. It didn't fit with what the book said, but why should it? It was just a dream-a stupid, awful dream. Jolie shut the book carefully, as if the knowledge it contained might leak out somehow. In the bed Jamie began to snore lightly, oblivious.

Despite telling herself that the dream was stupid-something to look past rather than deeper into-her fury that he would have lied, that he would have hidden the very information she had asked him for when they'd first met, burned hot. Stomping over to the kitchen she started a fresh pot of coffee. By the time it was ready she'd cooled down enough to sit and think things through.

Perhaps he had brought the book home to show her and forgotten, she forced herself to admit. If that was the case, he'd remember soon. But if he hadn't? If he had lied to her, it only made sense that he'd done so for a reason. He and Greta both were interested in fairies, maybe he thought her dreams actually had some significance. Oddly, she realized, she hadn't had one on any night he'd spent at her apartment.

She recalled the plate of cookies left out on the back steps of Gingerbread. Greta seemed to be trying to lure fairies to her. Her stomach twisted as she began to wonder why Jamie had gotten her the job at Gingerbread in the first place. She'd mentioned her dream right off. If it seemed significant to him, was that the whole reason he'd helped her, the reason Greta had been willing to hire her so quickly? If they thought her dream was significant, why hadn't they told her so? She knew they were up to something, and despite Greta's recent revelations she didn't think they planned on letting her in on the whole story. At least Greta didn't. She'd used Jolie to get to the cottage, she would use her again if she needed to. But Jamie hadn't known about that. How complicit was he?

To distract herself she found a scarf to wrap

her deck in, as Jamie had instructed, then lay on the couch to read the tarot book. At some point Boots appeared from points unknown, staring at her with appraising eyes before curling up in her lap. She passed out, waking in the morning to the sound of Jamie's groan.

"You conked out last night," she said, looking at him from the doorway, "want some coffee?"

He nodded, yawning hugely. "Would you get me some aspirin too, darlin'? I was tippling on some whiskey early in the day, think it caught up to me," he said, with a guilty smile.

She nodded, feeling guilty herself.

She drank coffee with him in bed, the two of them gazing out the small window, watching the white clouds creep across a swath of blue sky. At some point, despite the coffee, she fell back asleep, and when she woke Jamie was gone, a note on the counter saying he'd gone to Illuminations to try and make some money. She chewed her lip as she read the note, surprised he'd go back there after Bella had informed him the cops had been around. He was either lying, or broke enough to take a risk. Both seemed equally possible.

He didn't return that day, or that evening. Alone in bed that night Jolie realized that, despite her doubts about him, she had become dependent on Jamie's physical presence. The warmth and smell of him had comforted her more than she'd known; alone in bed she felt scared of the darkness, of the dream waiting to claim her.

§

Halloween.

Jolie woke as though someone had whispered the word in her ear a moment before.

"Shit!" she said, jumping out of bed. She was running late, although not impossibly so. Jamie's side of the bed was still empty, the sight made her heart ache. Despite everything, she felt he was one of the only people who had ever seen the real her. She did not want to continue through life unseen, hidden beneath a mask of others' expectations, hidden by their blindness. Hurrying to dress, she wiped away the hot tears that slid down her cheeks.

The forest was a dark tunnel lined in ruby and garnet leaves, the colors glowing strangely in the early, storm choked light. The rain had not yet begun but she could breathe it in, the air moist and thick. At the lake she stopped, despite her lateness, and walked towards the shore. Down by the water was a small boat, just a lightweight canoe, tied to a tree by a thick length of rope.

She almost got in and untied the rope. The longing in her to do this defied reason, scared her even. She ran the rest of the way to work feeling upended, her thoughts like a bag of marbles that had ripped open.

§

Greta wore all black, her skin almost glowing in contrast. Her hair was braided then wrapped around her head, her smile wide with excitement as she greeted Jolie. Jolie had thrown on her favorite gray cardigan, realizing her tarot deck was in the pocket only when it bounced uncomfortably against her leg as she ran. She'd had no thought to dress up although, feeling as she did, a mask might've been nice.

"Halloween!" Greta said, then did a little heel clicking dance. Jolie felt her false grin tremble.

"Jamie's gone. He left late yesterday morning to read cards and never came back."

"What?" Greta's expression changed dramatically. "He's *missing*?" Throwing a pan of cookies in the oven she picked up the phone, dialed.

"Hi Bella. Sorry, I know it's early. Is Jamie there? Seems like he might be MIA. Did you see him yesterday?"

Jolie watched her brow furrow, her lips tighten.

"You know, I'm doing the Halloween festival today, but I'd give you the money if you have time to do the honors." She paused. "Great. See you soon."

Greta turned back to Jolie, looking slightly relieved. "He's in jail. But I'm going to bail him out. Or Bella is, once she gets her fat ass out of bed. I can't believe she didn't call me earlier!"

Jolie didn't say anything, didn't point out that she was his girlfriend, that someone might have called her.

"Thanks for bailing him out," she said, finally, then put an apron on and got to work.

§

Jolie pressed the metal witch cookie cutter into the sugar dough, wondering again why Greta had wanted her out of commission at the cottage. Had she accomplished whatever she'd hoped to do? The two women performed a sort of dance, putting baking sheets in the oven, taking them out, skipping over to the pantry, glancing at the clock, whipping batter, frosting cakes. Greta would glance at her every once in a while, offer a distracted smile, then go back to transferring cakes into boxes, singing softly under her breath.

Jolie figured she'd find out more by pretending to know nothing. So she watched, played dumb, and returned the distracted smiles of the woman she now trusted not at all.

Bella stopped by an hour after the phone call. Greta handed her an enormous wad of cash, not even stopping to count it. Bella's eyes widened at the green bills spilling out of her hand. She looked ready to say something but Greta, who had already returned to cake frosting, said, "Hurry. Please." Bella clamped her lips shut on whatever question had been forming and left with a nod.

"Can't think of a day he'd less want to be in jail," Greta said, smiling as if it were amusing.

Jolie pressed the cookie cutter in so hard it bent.

§

By the time they got to the festival it was mid-afternoon and they were late. Greta directed her to carry things to a table under the main tent; someone had already set up bowls of cider and towers of red plastic cups for them. Greta arranged the pastries, waiting until a small hungry mob had gathered before unveiling her piece de resistance: the cemetery cake with vanilla wafer tombstones. Skeletal limbs made of thin white piping crawled out of the graves. It was artfully done; they'd been so busy Jolie hadn't seen it finished until now. She was about to compliment

Greta on her work when Jamie ran up to them, easily parting the crowd with his alarming appearance.

"Greta, it's a masterpiece!" Jamie said, looking drunk on freedom, enveloping Jolie in a hug.

"You deserve the first slice, after they day you've had," Greta replied. Pulling a huge knife out, she cut the cake into sections and gave him a corner piece. All around the outside of the table children's hands shot up, asking for the next slice. Greta grinned, eyes alight, and started handing out plates. Jamie turned to Jolie, offering her the first bite, but she shook her head and pulled him to her. She didn't know it was going to happen until it began, the sobs silent but racking. She felt Jamie turn and give Greta a look before he led her under the tent flaps and out onto the relative privacy of the green.

"I missed you," he said, his dark gaze sincere. Her sobs only grew harder as he placed the cake on the ground and pulled her into a kind of crouched huddle with him. She knew they must be a strange sight but couldn't care.

After a few minutes she wiped her eyes, sat down on the grass.

"You must be hungry," she said, nodding towards the cake. He nodded, looking guilty.

"Starved," he said, and wolfed down the cake

in under a minute. Wiping frosting from his lips, he pulled her to her feet and wrapped an arm around her waist.

"Greta can handle things by herself for a while. Let's go enjoy the festival," he said. She didn't argue. Feeling like someone just released herself, and unsure if her freedom would last, she followed him back into the tent. People swirled around them; parents carrying pumpkin-costumed babies, dozens of young witches, and a group of twenty-somethings in Renaissance garb. They stood for a moment before a dunk tank where adolescents threw baseballs at a bulls-eye, an older man who looked like a school principal taunting them about their aim. When the taunts were silenced with a splash they moved on, gravitating towards the animals. Farmers from the county had brought in their prize-winning smaller livestock; roosters crowed their challenges and lambs bleated bland complaints. One of the roosters seemed to take exception to Jamie, thrusting its head forward aggressively and staring him in the eye as though daring him to make the first move. Jamie laughed, moving his head from side to side like a boxer about to spring. Jolie almost managed a smile. Turning slightly, two little black goats in the farthest corner of the tent caught her eye and she walked over to them, leaving Jamie with his feathered foe. They came right over to her, butted her hands with their velvety heads until she stroked them between the ears, gazing into their strange eyes.

They'd almost made a full circuit of the crowded tent when Jolie saw the shock of white hair.

"Jamie," she whispered, tugging his sleeve. Looking up she saw him staring at Horace, who was buying a drink from the red and white soda stand.

"He's the one," Jamie whispered, and she tugged his sleeve again to get him to stop staring. Eyes wide with anger, he looked at her. "He's the one who ratted me to the police. He's trying to sabotage us."

"Sabotage? Jamie, what are you talking about?"

He started to bound off into the crowd but she grabbed his arm, using all her strength to hold him.

"Stop! What are you planning to do? Fight him in the middle of all these people? I don't want you getting thrown in jail again, ok?" Her voice surprised her by breaking at the end. He looked around, noticed that a small circle was being created around them, parents avoiding eye contact as they gave them a wide berth.

"You're right," he said, putting a lid on his anger. "Let's go talk to Greta. We need a plan."

Back at the table Greta was flushed and nearly

out of goodies.

"I think the planning board seriously underestimated the number of sugar fiends in this town," she said, wiping her brow with the back of her hand. The two joined her behind the table.

"He's here," Jamie said. "Horace."

"Shit," she hissed.

"And you know what?" Jamie's voice was angry and hard, each word blunt as a brick. "Bet he called the cops on me. Cause he wants to stop us."

At this Greta glanced at Jolie, as if trying to gauge what she made of this comment.

"Let's get out of here and talk," Greta said. "I'm basically done anyway." She started putting the remaining food on plates and packing her containers in bags. She'd almost finished when Horace appeared out of the crowd, materializing in front of Greta with a sharp smile on his face.

"I'd so wanted to talk to you," he said. Looking over the table he drew his eyebrows together in a parody of hurt and disappointment. "You're not leaving, are you?"

Greta seemed to turn ever whiter, which Jolie hadn't thought was possible.

"Get away from me, Horace."

He held up his hands, palms towards her.

"Just wanted to know if you have any special plans for this evening."

Greta was baring her teeth at him when Jamie shouldered her out of the way to take his turn staring down Horace.

"Leave us alone...or else."

Horace chuckled, tipped his hat.

"I'll be seeing you...sooner than later, I think." He turned and, whistling, began to saunter off. Greta's face went from white to red.

"That song he's whistling, he used to play that album when we had sex." She looked young, suddenly, like a scared child. If it hadn't been for the poisoned cookie Jolie would have felt terribly sorry for her.

Jamie put his hand on the small of Greta's back and gave her a gentle push towards the tent flap. Shaking herself out of it she picked up some of the bags and stepped outside. Jamie, carrying the rest, followed her. Jolie stood watching the white hair disappear into the crowd before turning and joining the others hurrying to Greta's car. Jamie sat up front, turning in his seat once they were in motion so he could face them both.

"It had to have been him, smug, elitist bastard. So, what are we going to do?" he asked Greta.

"Why do you think he called the cops on you?" Jolie asked. "Does he even know your name? And what is he trying to stop you from doing?"

Jamie looked at Greta, who looked at Jolie in the rear-view mirror.

"We're trying to work some magic, tonight. It makes sense he would try to get Jamie out of the picture. He knows I can't do it by myself so if Jamie were gone I might be forced to accept his help. And if I didn't accept his help, at least he would have sabotaged me. He wins either way, just in varying degrees." Greta glanced down at the clock. "We've got about three hours until dark. We just need to steer clear of him for that long." She sounded more determined than afraid, but her hands held the steering wheel like it might decide to steer her into traffic at any moment.

"What kind of magic?" Jolie asked. In her mind, she heard the thunder of the storm over the water, felt waves pitch beneath her. She took a deep breath. Again, Jamie deferred to Greta.

"We're going to wait until the veil between the worlds is thinnest," Greta said, glancing at the cars stopped nearby them at a red-light, presumably watching for Horace, "and then we're going to open a door."

"A door to...?"

"He knows where we're going to be," Jamie interrupted her question as they turned onto Greta's street. "Jolie saw him in the woods, and then he found you two at the cottage before."

Greta's lips pursed. "I know," she said. "You're right. We'll have to be ready for him."

§

Greta parked in her driveway. A young mother sat on the front steps next door, putting makeup on a young boy dressed as a vampire. She grinned and waved at them. The three of them waved back, Jolie's hand feeling wooden, only remotely attached.

Inside Greta led them to the living room. Jolie hadn't seen much of the house beyond the kitchen and bathroom, entering this room she wondered if Greta had bought the place furnished. The chairs, lamps, and tables seemed of a period, although poorly cared for; the cushions of all the seats had been rent by cat claws. The culprit sat curled up on an overstuffed plum colored chair, her eyes opening only to slits as they came in, luxuriously unconcerned.

"She looks like a little furry dragon," Jolie said, and the other two, miles away in thought, took a moment to realize what she was even saying.

Belatedly, Jamie laughed. "Just as dangerous, I'm sure," he said, with a slight bow towards Strega.

Greta closed the thick red drapes and turned on the small lamps, covered in shades of multi-colored glass.

"What should we do about Horace?" she asked Jamie, sitting down on the chair nearest the cat, next to the fireplace. Jolie's gaze slid down the tilted mantle, across the painted floorboards, then back up to Jamie.

He was rolling a cigarette and looking at Greta for permission.

"Go ahead," she said, grabbing a tarnished silver bowl off a nearby cabinet and handing it to him.

He lit up, closed his eyes, inhaled deeply. "If we don't kill him, we're going to have to at least tie him up. He can't interfere." Jamie inhaled again, fell back against the clawed, ivory loveseat. "I've always thought of myself as a pacifist, but the thought of someone taking this away from me..." He shook his head, turned to Greta. "You got some rope around here, or duct tape maybe?"

She nodded, and stood as if to look for it.

When she left the room, Jolie went and sat next to Jamie.

"We're going to stay together, right?" she asked. "No matter what happens?"

He stroked her hair and she was embarrassed at how badly she wanted to lean into him, rub against him like a cat. His dark eyes were full of thoughts, absent.

"Of course, darling." He stroked her hair again, seeming to come into the present. "Greta needs you, too," he said, lowering his voice to a whisper. "We're all going through." He said it as if he might make it true by speaking it with enough conviction. Numb with the looming possibilities, Jolie leaned into him and closed her eyes.

§

At twilight, carrying packs loaded with food, candles, and clothing, they slipped into the woods. Jolie walked in front, Greta in the middle. Jolie tried to breathe quietly, to listen for whatever might sneak up behind them. The shadows seemed to pulse with something akin to light, the darkness alive with a strange vibrancy.

They reached the lake to find the full moon shining above it, its reflection almost identical on the still water. She watched Jamie and Greta pause to gaze at it, as though making a wish, before continuing to the canoe. Once in Greta and Jamie rowed, their paddles cutting softly into the dark water as if trying not to awaken something below.

Jamie pulled the boat onto the sandy clearing only a few yards from the cottage's front door. The three of them fanned out around the entrance, Jolie grabbing Jamie's hand as she took in the dark, silent house. His fingers rested limply in her palm before he noticed and squeezed her hand in return. He turned to her, a small hopeful smile on his face.

"You have to open the door," he told her.

"Why me?" Jolie asked, looking at the two of them watching her, expectant.

"Because the cottage appeared to you, not us," Greta said. She didn't succeed in keeping the envy from her voice.

"What happens once we're inside?" Jolie asked. The wind had picked up suddenly, whipping her hair into her face, wrapping them in the scent of wet, rotting leaves.

"We hope the witch appears, and guides us through to her world," Greta answered.

"The *witch...*?" Jolie asked.

"The one who saved me after the plane crash; the same one you've been seeing in your dreams," Greta said.

Jolie rounded on Jamie. "I never told Greta about my dreams! Couldn't you two have included me in your plans rather than whispering about me behind my back?"

Greta sighed impatiently. "Look, we only met you a couple of weeks ago. We had to be sure we could trust you."

She glared at Greta. "And do you trust me now? Or just need me?" Reaching out, she shoved the heavy wooden door as hard as she could, pretending it was Greta.

The three stood, gaping at the darkness within for several moments, until Greta whispered, "The lanterns!" and they each dug the glass boxes out of their packs and lit the large candles within. The three small flames had the effect of making the night beyond even darker.

"I know flashlights would have been simpler," Greta said, "but I don't think they'll work in the other place, if we get through."

"Let's go!" Jamie whispered, and the excitement in his voice almost made Jolie smile. Holding her lantern high, she stepped over the threshold.

A moment later Jamie and Greta crowded in behind her, their lanterns helping to illuminate the walls made of wide wooden boards, the dirt floor, the huge fireplace.

"This looks like the summer kitchen for an old

manor home," Greta said, amused. She put her pack down on a table before the fireplace and dug out several candles. The room came into greater focus as she lined the table with them; there was a narrow bed under the window to their left, a pile of pots and lids next to the fireplace. In the small space, even these items didn't dispel the feeling of emptiness; it felt as though no one had stepped foot in here for centuries.

Jamie moved in the direction of the bed, eyes wide as he looked over every inch of the one room cottage.

"So, you are working a spell..." Jolie began, but the crack of a branch outside put them all on alert. Jamie moved behind the door, and when Horace walked in, looking devilish in the flickering light, Jamie took him by surprise, pulling both arms behind his back.

"Hold him!" Greta said, "I'll tie him up." She dug through her bag as Horace twisted in Jamie's grip, nearly freeing himself twice, landing an elbow in Jamie's stomach that made the younger man look grim and nauseous.

"Greta, I can help you," Horace said, his tone merely that of someone distressed over a misunderstanding. "You know I can."

As she walked over to him, cautious that she

stay out of kicking range, he tried to catch her gaze. She averted her eyes, biting her lower lip as she looped the tape tightly around his wrists, the sound of the tape peeling from its roll like a rip in the fabric of the night.

Jolie stood by the fireplace, watching, unwilling to help them. She had no idea who Horace really was, she realized. Nothing Greta had said could be assumed to be true.

"Really? This is the thanks I get for my financial contribution?" He asked, turning to look over his shoulder as Greta wrapped the tape a final time, sarcasm thick on the last two words.

"Thanks," she said, looking at him finally.

Horace threw his head back in an attempt to head butt Jamie.

"We need to tape him to that chair," she said, as Jamie dodged the blow.

Greta brought a chair over from the table and kicked Horace behind the knees so he would sit. Jamie held him down once he was in place so she could tape his ankles to the chair legs, but he wouldn't stop moving them. Growling in frustration, she returned to her bag and pulled out the knife she'd cut the cemetery cake with earlier that day.

Taking Jamie's place behind Horace, Greta held the knife edge to his throat.

"Stay still," she said, nodding to Jamie to continue with the tape. In half a minute Horace was secure, the chair angled so he faced the fireplace.

Taking a deep breath, Greta pulled a bowl from her bag and filled it with cookies they'd made that day. She cut open a pomegranate and placed the red half circles, with their jewel-like seeds, on top of the cookies, then placed the bowl in the middle of the floor. Next, she pulled a bag of sugar from Jamie's pack, and around the bowl she poured the sugar in thick lines, the pentagram about five feet long and surprisingly symmetrical when she was finished.

"Why sugar?" Jolie asked, breaking the silence that had been thickening around them. Glancing behind her, she saw Horace craning over his shoulder to see what Greta was doing.

"Faeries love sweets," Horace offered, sounding oddly professorial for a bound man. "Greta is trying to lure her fairy here, though whether the sugar is the greatest lure..."

"Shut up, you old goat," Greta breathed through her mouth, crouched next to the pentagram, cutting Jamie's finger with the tip of the knife. He sucked in air as several drops of blood fell on the snowy expanse of sugar.

"You next," Greta said to Jolie.

Jolie hesitated, the sight of blood making her feel woozy.

"Why?" She demanded. "If you are offering it sugar why do you need blood?"

"We're offering it food," Jamie said, sucking his finger, and Jolie saw Greta shoot him a warning look.

"Really, Greta," Horace said. "You haven't even told her your story, have you?"

Greta's lips tightened, but after a moment she set the knife on the ground, sat down in the folds of her black dress.

"After the plane crashed my brother and I stuffed our pockets with packages of airline peanuts, and I led us out into the woods. After hours and hours, the sun still hadn't come out, but night hadn't come either. We walked though this impossible purple twilight. The trees were covered in blood red berries and improbable flowers. I hadn't consciously thought 'we're in another world,' but I had known.

"She found us shortly after Hank died, appearing out of the woods, painfully beautiful even with the yellow cat eyes and the too-sharp teeth. She wore a tattered cloak the color of dried leaves. At times she would dig in the snow on all fours, like an animal. She would call birds down from the sky and when they landed she might pet them or kill them for food, I never knew which she'd do. The woods were hers, the world, perhaps, was hers. I never saw another person there. She brought Hank's body back to her hut and cooked him. I stayed outside, focusing on the glow of the world around me, turning my thoughts outwards, always outwards. After a time, she brought me inside, gave me only water. All traces of my brother were gone, and during the rest of my time there I tried not to think of him. It was easy. I was enchanted by the world, had never felt so happy. The whole time I was there I ate nothing. After a while, the witch walked me far into the woods. When I heard voices I grabbed her hand, scared of them, not her. When I saw the group of cross country skiers-two men and two women in bright coats and snow goggles, I realized she meant to return me to my world and I started to cry, pleading with her not to make me leave. She didn't say anything, but I could tell by her look that I'd disappointed her somehow. I knew I wasn't what she'd been looking for. The next thing I knew the skiers were shouting amongst themselves, rushing towards me. When I looked back the witch was gone."

Greta's face was etched with this loss.

There was silence for a moment, then Horace cleared his throat.

"Let me offer an alternative version," he said, trying to catch her eye, then Jamie's. "Imagine two small children survive a plane crash in winter. Shortly after, the younger dies and the older sister, thinking she herself might die soon, resorts to cannibalism. Most people wait more than four or five days before resorting to this measure, but perhaps Greta was an exceptionally hungry child.

"During the time I taught Greta she told me the story she just told you. Unbeknownst to her, I investigated it. The plane did crash, and Greta was found by skiers, a week later, with the remains of her brother's body. Hardly surprising that the fragile psyche of a child might invent a witch, a vicious force of nature, like hunger itself, to take the blame for what befell Hank."

Greta curled her lip in disgust. "You know I'm telling the truth, otherwise why are you here?"

"And why'd you set the cops on me?" Jamie asked. "Trying to get me out of the way."

Jolie was looking at Jamie when Greta grabbed her hand, turned it palm upwards, and drew her knife along Jolie's wrist. She tried to scream, but there was no air in her lungs. Greta yanked her over to the sugar and let the blood fall on it. Jolie felt her head spinning as one point of the pentagram became immediately soaked in her blood.

"It's easier if you don't see it coming," Greta said, unapologetic.

"Greta!" Jamie rushed over. "We only needed a few drops!"

Greta rolled her eyes. "So you think."

Jolie yanked her tarot deck out of her pocket, struggling to undo the knotted handkerchief so she could tie it around her wrist.

"I'm so sorry," Jamie said, eyes wide with fear. Taking the handkerchief, he tied it tightly around the cut. It was drenched in moments.

"You're going to be ok," he said, but she knew he didn't believe it. He pressed her wrist, as he led her over to the wall by Horace, where she could lean against something.

"Jamie, we have to begin," Greta said, trying to keep impatience from her voice.

"We have to-you cut her wrist, Greta! We need to get her help!"

Greta's sigh sounded as though it came from a great distance. "You know how much this means to me. And I know how badly you want to get over there. Maybe the witch will help her, but first we have to call her to us. So come help me!"

Jamie held her hand, his eyes looking deep into

hers as if for an answer. She saw the shift in him, the moment when he decided that he had to give up on her.

"Hang in there," he said, letting her hand drop, but she could tell he had no hope.

"Jamie..." Jolie heard her voice crack, watched as though from far away as he took his place on the opposite side of the pentagram from Greta, leaving her. They began chanting ugly, unintelligible words as Jolie's mind began to swim. The tarot cards were still in her uninjured hand, and she tried to focus on them, the bright pictures like little doorways her mind could escape through.

"Greta said I believed her, or I wouldn't be here." Jolie's neck felt like a column of water as she turned to look at the man tied up just three feet away. He was looking at her, at the puddle of blood that was spreading from her wrist, his eyes black in the darkness. "And she's almost right. I believe there was a witch; I just don't know if it was separate from her. She thinks the witch came to her because she wanted Greta's brother, but I think she wanted Greta. The skiers who found them said in the police report that she had obviously started to cannibalize the boy. But I think the witch was living in her when she did it, had found a desperate creature, at the end of her known reality, and stepped inside."

Jolie tried to pay attention to his words, but the colors of the cards were so bright. She flipped through them as best she could with one hand. The Fool, the Magician, the High Priestess; she flipped to the end of the Major Arcana: the World. A woman danced in the air, stepping through an oval wreath in the sky.

Jolie's eyes felt heavy; through slits she watched as the cottage door opened, revealing a dark square of night outside. Summoning her remaining strength, she stood and walked towards the door on shaky legs, the moist wind seeming to pull her forward. With some dim awareness she knew that Horace was still talking to her, knew Jamie and Greta were still chanting. At the door she heard Horace say, "She's gone!" And then the door closed behind her with a thud of finality.

Outside the world had dimmed. Clouds covered the moon, the air tense with the humid promise of a storm. The cool air condensed on her as she walked to the water's edge and got into the canoe. She rowed to the middle of the lake before she realized her wrist had stopped its throbbing. Resting the oars in their holders, she unwrapped the handkerchief. The wound was healed, the sight of the unbroken skin sending chills running through her.

Thunder bellowed across the water as lightning touched its jagged finger to the roof of the cottage. From the darkness she watched the flames grow, slowly at first, then faster. Distantly, she heard screams. No figures appeared, silhouetted against the fire, escaping. The screams went on for a long time until, finally, quiet crept towards her over the water. Picking up the oars she rowed hard for shore.

Stepping out of the boat, Jolie found herself in a different place than the one they'd departed from only a few hours before. The path was gone; in the strange purple twilight, even the plants looked different. She walked deeper into the trees, finally coming to an impassable wall of thorns and roses, the red flowers glowing in the strange light. She reached out, hoping to part them and pass beyond, but they bent before her, creating an opening large enough to walk through. Their movement filled the air with a heady perfume, the cloying sweetness a sort of screen through which she viewed the vision before her.

Beyond the roses, several trees had bent and twisted around one another to form a crooked little house. The bark was black with damp, a greenish smoke rising from the chimney. The leaves of the trees glistened wetly, the layers of red and gold forming a

sort of thatched roof which lay low and heavy as a
brow above the round, black staring eye of the open
door.

Entering, she found Boots and Strega. Curled
together on a table they blinked at her, approving. She
rubbed each of their heads for a moment as she looked
around the room, peering down several of the dark,
twisting passages that led from this space into other
cottages, in other forests.

Above the fireplace was an old, broken piece of
mirror. She walked over to it, peered at her reflection
through the shadows. Her yellow, cat-like eyes had no
trouble seeing. Jolie's face looked back at her, the face
she had often watched gliding towards her across a
storm trampled lake. She looked different now, her
features subtly transformed, the wildness and power of
the witch finally shining through.

From the hollow in her back she pulled forth
the tarot deck. Spilling the cards out onto the table,
she smiled. She'd liked the way the cards had looked,
through Jolie's eyes. Each one like a strange, twisting
passage, doorways into stories as old as mankind,
almost as old as she herself.

Made in the USA
Columbia, SC
30 November 2019